Journey to the Center of the Earth

*Retold from the Jules Verne original
by Kathleen Olmstead*

Illustrated by Eric Freeberg

STERLING CHILDREN'S BOOKS
New York

STERLING CHILDREN'S BOOKS
New York

An Imprint of Sterling Publishing Co., Inc.
1166 Avenue of the Americas
New York, NY 10036

ISBN 978-1-4027-7313-6

Library of Congress Cataloging-in-Publication Data

Olmstead, Kathleen.
  Journey to the center of the earth / retold from the Jules Verne original by Kathleen Olmstead ;
illustrated by Eric Freeberg.
    p. cm. — (Classic starts)
  Summary: Professor Liedenbrock, his nephew Axel, and their guide Hans explore a volcanic
crater in Iceland that leads them to the center of the Earth and to incredible and horrifying
discoveries.
  ISBN 978-1-4027-7313-6
  [1. Explorers—Fiction. 2. Science fiction.] I. Freeberg, Eric, ill. II. Verne, Jules,
1828–1905. Voyage au centre de la terre. III. Title.
  PZ7.O515Jo 2011
  [Fic]—dc22

                                                                    2010009754

Distributed in Canada by Sterling Publishing Co., Inc.
$^c/_o$ Canadian Manda Group, 664 Annette Street
Toronto, Ontario, Canada M6S 2C8
Distributed in the United Kingdom by GMC Distribution Services
Castle Place, 166 High Street, Lewes, East Sussex, England BN7 1XU
Distributed in Australia by Capricorn Link (Australia) Pty. Ltd.
P.O. Box 704, Windsor, NSW 2756, Australia

For information about custom editions, special sales, and premium and corporate purchases,
please contact Sterling Special Sales at 800-805-5489 or specialsales@sterlingpublishing.com.

Manufactured in China
Lot#:
10 9
12/16

www.sterlingpublishing.com

CONTENTS

CHAPTER 1

An Old Book and a New Mystery

On May 24, 1863, my uncle rushed through the front door of our little house. Professor Liedenbrock, as my uncle was known, shared that small place with me in Hamburg, Germany.

"Axel," he shouted. "I need to speak with you!" He sped toward his study.

My uncle was often excited. A new idea or theory would send him rushing to his study to work. I was used to him acting this way. I had lived with him since I was a teenager—I was now twenty years old—so this was not new to me. He was an impatient man. He did not like to wait for anything.

This is the reason our housekeeper, Martha, panicked when Uncle Liedenbrock burst through the door. She assumed he wanted to have his supper. She rushed into the kitchen and said to me, "Axel, please don't tell him dinner isn't ready. Distract him. I'll have the meal on the table as soon as possible."

My uncle was not a bad man. In truth, he was just very odd. He taught mineralogy—the science of minerals—at the Johannaeum, the local university. However, he was not a good teacher. I also studied mineralogy at the university and had heard students complain about him.

He had very little interest in helping others learn. He was a very stubborn man and only talked about whatever interested him at the time. I heard stories about him flying into a rage if he thought a person misunderstood him.

He did not think that he needed to explain anything again or in a different way. When my uncle was misunderstood by anyone, he thought that that person simply was not listening.

Please keep in mind that my uncle was a scientist. He was a very smart man, and he was well respected. The Liedenbrocks were well known in Germany. There were many libraries and buildings with the family name. My uncle did not care about such things, though.

His entire life was wrapped up in his work. He was devoted to the study of minerals, rocks, and geography. He did worry about what other people thought of him. But he was just too occupied with his own scientific world to notice much else.

Therefore, Uncle Liedenbrock could not understand why I was so slow to follow him to his study. I thought I walked very quickly when he called. But it was not fast enough for him.

"What on earth took you so long? Do you expect me to wait all day?" My uncle was already sitting in his armchair. He had a very big book in his lap. He did not look up at me while he spoke.

I did not sit down right away, but stood by his desk. Uncle usually had a job for me to do. He might ask me to get a book down from a shelf. Or he could ask me to run into town to pick something up.

"What a book," he said. "What a book!" He shook his head in amazement. "Can you not see? This is a priceless gem I found in a shop this morning."

I gazed at the book in my uncle's hands. He carefully leafed through the pages. It looked old and tattered to me. I could see nothing special about it.

"What is the book about?" I asked. It was the only thing I could think to say.

"It is an Icelandic book from the twelfth

century," he said. "It is the story of Norwegian princes ruling Iceland."

"But Uncle," I said. "Can you read Icelandic?"

"Icelandic? Yes, a little. But Axel, you are a fool," Uncle Liedenbrock said. "This is not written in Icelandic. It is written in runes."

"Runes?" I gasped. I ran to his side to look at the book more closely.

The pages were filled with small stick-like figures. The language looked impossible to understand, and I was not very interested in learning it. My uncle, however, had a lot to say on the subject.

Uncle Liedenbrock described to me the history of the runic language. It was used mostly in Iceland and other northern countries. He told me this book was handwritten and one of a kind.

This speech could have gone on for hours. But one thing stopped it. A piece of paper fell from the book and landed by my uncle's feet.

5

Liedenbrock quickly reached down and grabbed it. "What is this?" he said, studying it.

He walked over to his desk. He very carefully laid the paper down. It was five inches wide and three inches long. The page was filled with runes.

"Whatever does it mean?" my uncle said.

This was such an important question. Little did we know that the answer would soon lead us on the adventure of a lifetime.

CHAPTER 2

Uncle Liedenbrock Works Night and Day to Solve the Mystery

∾

Before he did anything else, my uncle had to translate the note. It was all he could think about. He was certain it held a secret. He was determined to discover it.

Uncle Liedenbrock tried translating the runes into Icelandic. It did not work. Then he tried translating it into Latin. Again, nothing.

"It is written in a code," he said. "I'll have to solve the code to read the message."

He pronounced to me all the letters in the Icelandic alphabet. On a piece of paper, I lined them up beside each letter in our alphabet. We then used that as a code to crack the runes's message. We changed all of the Icelandic letters in the message to our letters to see what it would spell. Nothing! It was all gibberish. Uncle picked up the parchment and held it beside the book.

"The handwriting is different," he declared. "The book and the note were not written by the same people! Someone must have written this note then left it tucked inside."

"But how can we know who used to own the book?" I asked.

Uncle Liedenbrock sat down at his desk and pulled the book close to him. Using a magnifying glass, he examined each page. Finally, he found something. He saw two words spelled out in runes. But this time, my uncle could translate the words.

"Arne Saknussemm!" he declared. "Arne Saknussemm wrote his name in the book!"

"Who?" I asked. I was very confused.

"He was a very famous Icelandic writer of the sixteenth century. He was a great scientist and explorer."

"Why would he hide his name in the book?" I asked. "Why would he write his name in runes and not Icelandic?"

My uncle waved his hand at me as if my question was ridiculous.

"How would I know such things? The why is not important to me," he said. "My only concern is reading this message. I can read runes, but these are all mixed up. We must think about nothing else until the mystery is solved!"

"Should we wait until after dinner?" I asked my uncle.

"No distractions!" he said. "We will not eat or sleep until we have the answer."

While Uncle Liedenbrock tried to crack the code, I stared at the picture above the fireplace.

It was of Gräuben. She was a young woman in town who had no father. She was a ward of my uncle. This meant my uncle took care of her. Gräuben was also my fiancée.

Gräuben was a blond, smart, and slightly serious young woman. I was amazed that someone so perfect could love me. No one knew we were engaged, though. Not even my uncle. It was not something he would understand.

"Axel!" my uncle cried. His shout awoke me from my daydream.

He was surrounded by more books and more pieces of paper than before. He had been trying code after code.

"I need you to write out a sentence for me. Any sentence." He handed me paper and pen without looking up.

"Do not write it from left to right. Write it top to bottom so there are five columns."

I did as I was asked.

l	y	y	l	u
l	o	l	e	b
o	u	i	G	e
v	,	†	r	n
e	m	†	ä	

"Excellent!" my uncle said. He snatched the paper and went to work. He did not really see what I had written.

"Now let's read the words from left to right." He rewrote my message in this way. Then he read it out loud. "Iyylu loleb ouiGe v,trn emtä."

My uncle stared at the paper for a few minutes. He then said, "I love you, my little Gräuben." He had finally seen what I wrote. He did not sound surprised or amazed. "So, you are in love with Gräuben?"

"Um, y-yes," I stuttered.

"Let's see if this code works with the runes in the note," he said. Nothing more was said about

Gräuben and me. My uncle went to work again, but had no success. He threw his pen down in great disgust.

"That's not it! This makes no sense. It must translate into Latin, as that is the language of scholars. But still, I can make no sense of it."

He stood up from his desk and shot across the room like a cannonball. He was out of the house in seconds. I had no idea where he had gone.

I sat quietly in my chair not knowing when my uncle would return. I thought of taking a nap. I thought of reading one of the other books on the shelves. In the end, I decided it was best to wait.

I remained in the chair with the piece of paper in my hand. I hoped that my uncle solved the mystery—or tired of it—soon. We would be like prisoners in the house until it was over.

I held the piece of paper before me, waving it like a fan. I was not really concentrating on it, and I was not trying to read the code. However, I must have taken in more than I realized. Maybe it was easier to read when I was not trying so hard, because suddenly the answer came to me. I just understood all its secrets.

I also knew that my uncle should never see this note. It told of a journey that few would believe. But I knew my uncle would insist on making this journey if he read this note. He would surely take me with him. But I did not want to go. I did not want to risk never seeing Gräuben again.

I told myself I would destroy the note. Standing by the fire, my hand held the note above the flames. I was about to drop it in when I heard my uncle returning to his study. There were only a few seconds to get the note back to his desk as if nothing had happened.

CHAPTER 3

Axel Has a Secret

I moved very quickly. The note was back in its place before my uncle closed his office door. He did not notice anything strange.

As it turned out, Uncle Liedenbrock had only gone for a walk. He was trying to clear his head. He said he wanted to return to the work with "fresh eyes." Unfortunately, this was not the case. In fact, my uncle continued to struggle for many hours.

I did feel guilty! Honestly, I did. However, I

felt it was for the best—for his safety and mine—if I kept the secret to myself.

I stayed with my uncle, though. I answered his questions and listened to his theories and suggestions. I tried to get him to eat something (I failed) and encouraged him to drink some water.

In those first few hours, I was certain he would discover the truth. After all, how could I have been successful while my brilliant uncle struggled?

By midnight, though, I saw that he was trying too hard. The answer was really very simple. He was missing it entirely. When I was no longer worried about him discovering the secret, I fell asleep.

When I woke up in the morning, my uncle was still working. He looked exhausted. There were dark circles under his eyes. He stooped over his desk as he scribbled his notes.

Martha tried to leave the house for her morning trip to the market. She found the front door locked. The key was not in the lock as it usually was. Without the key, we would remain locked inside!

My uncle must have absentmindedly put it in his vest pocket. I tried asking him about the key, but he would not listen. He could concentrate on nothing but his precious note. Several more hours passed, and I started to feel desperate. By midafternoon, I was starving.

My uncle stood up, announcing he was off for another walk. I knew this meant that he might lock us inside again. I didn't know when he would return or when I might eat. I knew that I had to act.

"Uncle," I said. He did not hear me. "Uncle!" I repeated loudly. There was still no response. "Uncle Liedenbrock!" I yelled. This time he turned toward me. "What about the key?" I asked.

"What, boy? The key?" he asked. He was truly confused by my question.

"The key to the message," I said. "What about the key to the message?"

My uncle's eyes grew large.

"What are you saying?" His voice was low, but excited. I had never seen him like this before.

I picked up the note and whispered, "Look. Read."

He shook his head in disbelief. "No," he said. "It doesn't make sense."

"Yes," I said again. "It does when you begin at the beginning." I pointed to the last word in the message. "Start here and read the message backward."

My uncle snatched the note from my hand. It only took a moment or two before he realized what I meant. He let out a wild whoop!

"Oh, you clever Saknussemm!" he cried. "You wrote your message backward!"

17

Uncle Liedenbrock sat back down and quickly wrote out the message.

Go down the crater of the volcano Snaefells. Follow the shadow just before the month of July. You will find your way to the center of the Earth. I did it.
Arne Saknussemm.

My uncle reacted as I thought he would. He paced across the room. He held his head in his hands and talked to himself. Every once in a while, he let out a great yelp of excitement.

"Axel," he said. "We'll have to get to it."

"Get to what?" I asked.

"Packing," he nearly yelled. "We're going to Iceland to the volcano Snaefells. We are going to follow the path to the center of the Earth!"

CHAPTER 4

Axel Worries About the Future

୶

I was not as excited by this trip as my uncle was. In fact, I was frightened and did not want to go. The risks were too great. We might never return. I might never see my Gräuben again.

For Uncle Liedenbrock, though, there was only excitement. This journey would lead to the greatest scientific discovery ever. He insisted we keep our journey a secret. He was certain that someone would try to steal our glory.

"Uncle," I said. "Do you really think that anyone else would attempt this journey?"

"Definitely," he said. "Who would refuse? Every scientist would jump at the chance."

"How do we know that this is not a practical joke?" I asked. "How do we know that it is real?"

At first I thought I had upset my uncle. He looked angry. But then he smiled.

"I guess we will soon find out," he said. If my uncle was a different person, he might have winked. His smile showed his good spirits.

"But what if the volcano is still active? It would be very dangerous to walk into a volcano that is about to erupt." I was trying to find any excuse that might change his mind.

"Once again, we won't know until we get there," Uncle Liedenbrock said. "You must remember, Axel, that more volcanoes in the world are quiet than active. The odds are in our favor that it will be extinct. Snaefells has not erupted since the year 1219."

"But Uncle," I said. "What about the theory

that the Earth's core is boiling hot? At two hundred thousand degrees, everything—rock, gold, silver—turns into gas. We would be fine for the first hundred feet. But the heat will increase farther on."

"How could we know what happens at the Earth's core?" Uncle Liedenbrock asked. "We have only explored a very small portion of it. Theories are only theories until they are proved true. Some scientists, including myself, think it's not true that the Earth's core is boiling hot."

As always, it was impossible to argue with my uncle. Despite his strange ways, Uncle Liedenbrock was good to me. He let me live with him while I went to the university. He included me in his research projects. I knew that I was lucky to work with such a brilliant scientist. If only our work kept us safely at home!

"Don't you see the opportunity that we have, Axel?" My uncle put his hand on my arm. "Out of all these theories made by all these scientists, we will be the ones to find the truth."

"Yes!" I said. I was starting to feel his excitement. "We can do this! We can be the first!" I left his study confident that we would succeed.

Unfortunately, this feeling did not last. While my uncle thought he could never make a wrong step, I worried about each and every one. It did not take long before I was back to worrying about what might happen. By the time I reached Gräuben, I was in a state of panic.

She noticed immediately that something was troubling me.

"Axel," she said sweetly. "What is wrong?"

Although I had promised Uncle Liedenbrock that I would tell no one, I could keep no secrets from Gräuben. I gave her all the details.

"Oh, Axel," she said. She touched her fingertips to my cheek. "It will be a wonderful journey."

I almost jumped a mile. A *wonderful* journey? Did I hear her correctly?

"Listen to me," Gräuben said. She knew I was nervous and was trying to calm me down. "You are the nephew of a great man. You are just as worthy as he is. This is your opportunity to prove yourself. This will be a great adventure."

"But Gräuben," I said. "I thought you would try to stop me. It is going to be a dangerous journey, you know."

"I know, dear Axel. It will be hard, but you will learn so much. When you return, you will be able to tell the world all the incredible things you have seen. You will be the first, and you should be proud. I wish I had the same opportunities as you."

I was shocked and amazed. Not only was Gräuben not trying to stop me—she was actually excited for me! Gräuben's faith restored me. She loved me and wanted me to go on this journey. More and more, I realized how lucky I was to have Gräuben in my life. I was still scared, but I felt stronger thanks to her love.

When I returned home, my uncle was busy packing. There were many men walking through the house. They were carrying in supplies and helping to pack. My uncle's two suitcases and boxes of equipment were in the hallway. Martha was rushing about, trying to get things done. Uncle Liedenbrock was directing everyone.

"Uncle?" I said. "I was only gone a few hours. How did you get so much done so quickly?"

"We are leaving, my boy!" Liedenbrock said. "We're leaving the day after tomorrow, at the crack of dawn. There's so much to do!"

"Why must we hurry?" I asked. "Do we have to leave so soon?"

"Do you think it is easy to get to Iceland? We have a long train ride. Then we must find a boat to take us to the island, which is in the middle of the Atlantic Ocean. Once there, we must hike to the volcano. And we must do it all before July. We do not have much time."

"But it is only May 26—" I started to say.

"Axel, why aren't you helping?" my uncle

said, cutting off my words. "You must organize your things. We must leave on time!"

The next day, more and more supplies arrived. The men strapped them down to a wagon as my uncle supervised. Everything was prepared to take us to the train station.

The next morning, we got to the train station at dawn. I was very tired. My night had been filled with nightmares of dark tunnels and endless pits. I was very glad that Gräuben came along to see us off. But I worried it would be the last time we saw each other.

As always, my Gräuben did a fine job of calming me down. She kissed me on the cheek, then said, "I will make a promise to you, Axel. You are leaving a fiancée here in Germany but you will come back to a wife. When you return, I will marry you."

With that, I gave Gräuben a long hug and we were off.

CHAPTER 5

The Great Adventure Begins

જ્જ

We were riding the train toward Copenhagen, Denmark. From there, we would find a boat to take us to Iceland. I would have been happy if we never reached our destination. My uncle was constantly anxious that we were not moving fast enough.

If the train slowed down at all—even to stop at stations—my uncle became quite upset. He found the train conductor and demanded to know why there was a delay. The conductor explained they needed to let other passengers on and off. Uncle Liedenbrock thought that was a very poor excuse.

Our train ride to Copenhagen was broken up by a boat ride across a channel, or small body of water. This was particularly difficult for my uncle. He could not understand why the boat's captain did not set off right away. Why must we wait for the scheduled departure time? Why must we wait for other passengers to arrive? The captain advised my uncle to go for a walk.

On the other side of the channel, we still had to take another train before we reached Copenhagen, the capital city of Denmark. Thankfully, it was not a long ride.

My uncle had arranged a meeting with a professor at the university. This made for a very warm welcome! Professor Thomson was very helpful. He showed us around his city and said he would help us hire a boat to take us to Iceland.

I hoped there would be nothing available.

If we couldn't get to Iceland before the end of June, then the trip would be canceled. I was not so lucky, though. We found a boat leaving on June 2.

My uncle was very excited by this news. He shook the captain's hand so hard I thought he might break it. The captain found it quite normal to go to Iceland. That was his job. But my uncle thought it was incredible.

We had a few days to spend in Copenhagen before the boat sailed. I entertained myself by walking through the city, visiting museums and churches. I wished that my Gräuben was with me. We would have had a lovely time together. We could have walked over the beautiful bridges and toured the Royal Palace. Thinking about Gräuben only made me sad. I wondered if I would ever see her again.

The time finally came when we were due to leave. On June 2, at six in the morning, we loaded our luggage onto a small boat that would take us to Iceland.

The captain and crew greeted us as we walked onto the boat. They shook our hands then quickly went to work setting sail. Minutes later, we were heading out of the harbor.

According to our captain, the trip would take ten days. This was too long for my uncle, but he accepted it. He tried to keep himself busy by carefully planning our journey into the volcano.

Unfortunately, weather at sea was not in our favor. After only a few days, we were hit by a terrible storm. Off the coast of Scotland, the winds started to pick up. Soon the sky was black with clouds. Our boat began rolling in the high waves. We could not go on deck for two days because of the rain and wind. Even Uncle Liedenbrock was shaken up.

When we finally reached Iceland's shore, we had been at sea for thirteen days.

CHAPTER 6

A Warm Welcome to Iceland

∾

My uncle came out from his cabin a little blurry-eyed, but excited. Much of our boat journey had been spent inside. Once we came back up to the deck, the bright sun was startling. Uncle Liedenbrock was happy, though. There was a wide grin across his face. I realized how rarely my uncle smiled. It was nice to see.

He dragged me to the front of the boat and pointed north. "Axel, look there!" he said. A large mountain loomed before us. At the top of the mountain there were two points.

"It is Snaefells," he said. "That is the volcano that will lead us to the center of the Earth!" My uncle's excitement was catching. Even I was starting to feel eager for our adventure!

One of the first people to greet us on land was Baron Trampe. He was the governor of Iceland. Governor Trampe was expecting us. My uncle had sent a letter to him ahead of our arrival. The governor gave us a very warm greeting. He also offered to escort us through the city.

My uncle had to translate this information to me. He did not speak Icelandic well. I could not speak it at all. Thankfully, many people in Iceland also spoke Danish. Uncle Liedenbrock could speak with them this way. My uncle had to translate everything for me. Unfortunately, he was often too busy for this, leaving me to guess what people were saying.

The only person I could understand was Professor Fridriksson. He taught science at the

university and spoke Latin. I could understand Latin well, so I felt comfortable with him. Thankfully, he was also our host. We stayed at his home and shared wonderful meals with him.

Reykjavik, Iceland's capital, was a small and lovely place. On our first day there, I went on a walking tour. All the buildings in the city were quite simple. The town hall looked more like a country cottage. The school and churches were small and plain, but I found them beautiful.

While I explored our surroundings, Uncle Liedenbrock explored books. He had spent the whole day in the library. He was shocked by how few books he had found. That night, he complained about this to our host.

"My word!" Professor Fridriksson exclaimed. "We have eight thousand books to choose from."

"But where are they kept?" my uncle asked. "The shelves in the library were mostly bare."

"Why, all over the country, of course!"

Fridriksson said. "We are a country of readers. Books travel from home to home so we can all enjoy them."

"Now," Fridriksson said, "you only have to tell us what you would like to read. Then we can find it and have it sent to you."

My uncle did not have to think about this for long. He had his answer right away.

"Arne Saknussemm!" he said. In fact, he almost shouted the name. "I would love to read anything that great man wrote."

"Do you mean the Icelandic scientist and traveler?" Fridriksson asked.

"Yes, precisely," Liedenbrock replied.

"He was one of the greatest men to come from Iceland," Fridriksson continued. "He was a true genius and a truly courageous man."

"I see you know exactly who I mean," Uncle said. He was getting very excited. It was wonderful that our host also admired Saknussemm.

Fridriksson suddenly looked disappointed, though. "I'm afraid that we do not have any of his books," he said. "In fact, there are no books written by that great man available."

"What!" Uncle Liedenbrock cried. "No books? Not even in Iceland?"

"I'm afraid not." Fridriksson slowly shook his head. "All of his books were destroyed hundreds of years ago. It was at a time when the government—not in Iceland, but in Denmark—was frightened by ideas that were different from their own. So, to try to stop his ideas from reaching the people, they destroyed all his writings."

"Of course," my uncle shouted. "It all makes perfect sense! This explains why he had to write about his discovery in a code. He felt that he had to hide it."

"I don't understand," Fridriksson said. "Have you found something written by Saknussemm?"

"No, no," Uncle Liedenbrock stuttered, catching himself. "I was just thinking . . . he must have had to be so careful with his writing. It must have been hard for him." He had remembered, just in time, that our journey must remain a secret. He had almost revealed everything to our kind host! My uncle was not a good liar. He quickly changed the subject instead.

"We were wondering about the volcano, Snaefells," Liedenbrock said. "My nephew and I would like to study it. We are interested in collecting rocks for our research."

"Yes, of course," Fridriksson said. "You mentioned that in your letter. Well, the volcano is extinct, so you should be quite safe. There hasn't been an eruption for more than five hundred years."

"That is a relief," my uncle said. He was almost smiling again. I could tell that he was pleased by how well he had changed the subject.

"You will need a guide, though," Fridriksson said. "It is not easy to make your way up the mountain. And the crater in Snaefells has rarely been explored. Most of it is unknown. You will need someone with a lot of experience. I have just the man for you."

"That is very generous of you," Liedenbrock said. "Could I meet this man right away? Perhaps tonight, so we can start planning."

"Tomorrow," Fridriksson replied.

"I would prefer to talk to him tonight," Liedenbrock said. He was starting to become impatient. He forgot that he should be polite.

"Tomorrow," Fridriksson repeated. "He is a wonderful guide. But he is not someone you can rush. He will be here tomorrow."

"Very well, then," Liedenbrock said. "We will all meet tomorrow."

CHAPTER 7

A Guide for the Journey

ᮍ

I woke up the next morning to hear my uncle talking loudly in the next room. I quickly dressed and joined him.

Uncle was standing with a very tall and well-built man. He was the strongest-looking man I had ever seen. I watched this man with great interest. He moved slowly and carefully. His arms did not swing by his sides. All of his movements were controlled and exact. His eyes were blue and intelligent. He was like no one else I had ever met.

My uncle was speaking Danish to this man. I say "speaking to" rather than "speaking with" because Uncle Liedenbrock was doing all the talking. He only stopped when he saw me walk into the room.

"Axel, my boy," he said in German. "This is Hans. He will be our guide for the trip. He does not speak German, only Icelandic and Danish. You won't be able to talk to each other, but that's fine. Hans and I have already made all the necessary plans."

I nodded to Hans, and he nodded back. Despite our different languages, I knew we would get along just fine.

My uncle finally revealed his plan for the trip. Hans would lead us to the village of Strapi, just south of the volcano. It would take seven or eight days. We would have four horses, two for riding and two for luggage. Hans would walk. That is what he preferred. We would gather more supplies in Strapi, then start our climb up the volcano.

Hans agreed to work for my uncle until the journey was complete. Uncle Liedenbrock did not tell Hans our ultimate destination. I thought that he should be completely honest. But I knew my uncle had his reasons.

My uncle agreed to pay Hans every Saturday. It was understood that the contract would be broken if Hans was not paid on time.

We were to leave in two days. My uncle got to work packing and preparing right away. I worked alongside him, of course. My uncle spent much of his time packing all the instruments we would need. Many of them were delicate. He had to make sure they would not get damaged while traveling.

First of all, we had a special thermometer. It could read very high and very low temperatures. We also had an instrument to measure the air pressure. This instrument would tell us how much oxygen there was to breathe. We had to be careful as we headed so far underground. Then there was the chronometer. A chronometer is a very sturdy clock. We did not know what we might find on our journey. So we needed a timepiece that could work in very hot or very cold conditions. We carried two compasses. This would help us know in which direction we were walking. We packed three lanterns. Each was powered by a battery with an electrical charge that lit the bulb.

We also carried pickaxes, a hammer, a ladder made of silk, and lots of rope. Our food supplies were coffee, dried meats, crackers, nuts, and raisins. We had flasks, but we did not carry water. My uncle was sure we would find water along the way.

Before I knew it, two days had passed. We left for the volcano on June 16, at six in the morning.

The day was gray and overcast. We were pleased that there was no rain or severe heat. We had the perfect weather for tourists. Hans walked in front of us, and we followed on our horses.

Hans followed a route along the coast. It was very rocky, and we moved slowly. My uncle was growing impatient again. The trip was taking too long! He could not understand why we traveled at such a slow pace.

Uncle Liedenbrock tried to get his horse to move quicker. He dug his heels into the animal's sides. He flicked the reins. He leaned down on the horse's neck, hoping that would make it move. Nothing worked. The horse walked at the same pace that Hans did. It refused to go any faster unless Hans told it to.

We came to a river. It was about forty feet wide. Hans told my uncle, who then told me, that we would have to pause here.

My uncle did not wait to find out why we

were stopping or for how long. He clicked his heels into the horse's sides, forcing it into the water. He planned to cross the river and not wait for the rest of us.

The horse tried to turn back to the shore. My uncle did his best to stop him. They struggled, and my uncle lost. He was thrown from the horse's back into the river.

Thankfully, this happened not far from shore. My uncle could easily walk back. He looked embarrassed, so I did my best not to laugh. I also did not point out the approaching ferry. I realized then that Hans had brought us to a ferry stop. We got on, and it carried us along the river. Uncle Liedenbrock was soaking wet. He sat quietly on the ferry as it carried us safely to the other side.

CHAPTER 8

Snaefells, At Last

೧

It was late in the day by the time we reached the other side of the river. We only knew this by looking at the chronometer. The sky was still as bright as noon even though it was eight o'clock at night. Iceland is so far north that the sun never sets during June and July. It was hard going to sleep with the bright sun, but I got used to it.

Our slow but steady pace continued. I stopped whenever Hans told me to. I ate when he handed me food. The volcano was always in the distance, but it never seemed to get any closer.

Eventually, Hans led us to a farmhouse. He spoke with the farmer and his wife as we waited outside. Then he returned to us. He said we could sleep at the farmhouse that night and enjoy a bed for a change. I cannot explain how happy I was to hear this news. A bed! It seemed too good to be true.

I could not understand a word the farmer and his wife said. But I understood they were very generous. They made room for us even though they had nineteen children. They shared what little they had. We ate a dinner of soup, fish, and berries. I had a very peaceful sleep on a mattress filled with straw. It felt like heaven. I slept very well.

We left early the next day. The volcano was finally looking closer. At last I could see the progress we were making.

I was very happy when we finally arrived at the village of Strapi. The village was located at the foot of the volcano. It was wonderful knowing that the first part of our journey was done.

The village was very small. We traveled down the main street. People looked at us through their windows, but no one came out to greet us. I thought this was odd, yet who was I to judge? Perhaps they were not used to strangers visiting their town.

Hans led us to the rectory where the minister lived. Our guide asked if we could stay there while we prepared to climb the volcano. The minister spoke with his wife in private. When he came back, he agreed to our request.

The minister was not a friendly man. Neither he nor his wife smiled. They seemed to have no interest in conversation, either. There were no books in the house. They were not even interested in talking about books. My uncle decided we should leave as soon as possible.

He also decided that it was time to reveal

the full plan to Hans. My uncle told Hans that we would be traveling to the center of the Earth, and we were taking him with us. I expected our guide to react in anger or shock. Surely he would refuse to go on such a ridiculous journey. That did not happen. Hans just shrugged. It didn't matter to him where we went. He was hired as our guide. He would lead us wherever my uncle wanted to go.

I started to wonder what would happen as we walked into a volcano. Could we cause an eruption? If we did, we would be too far down to do anything about it. I mentioned my fear to my uncle. I expected an argument from him. Instead he stopped what he was doing and looked at me.

"Yes," he said. "I've thought of that, too."

I did not know what to say. He was thinking the same thing? Did that mean he was finally willing to turn back?

"I have investigated this. There are no signs

that an eruption will occur. We are quite safe. I promise."

Although I was still nervous, I took comfort in my uncle's words. After all, he was a very smart man.

Uncle Liedenbrock made arrangements with Hans. We would leave the minister's house early the next morning. I had a terrible night's sleep. My dreams were filled with explosions and danger. I knew this was my last chance to sleep in a bed for a long time. Still, I could not enjoy it.

The next morning, the horses were loaded and we were ready to leave. The minister handed my uncle a sheet of paper. It was a bill for our stay! Uncle Liedenbrock paid him without a second thought. He wanted to be on his way. It was best just to leave this place behind.

Once we left the village of Strapi, we approached the volcano. Snaefells was five thousand feet high. We stood at the base of the volcano and looked up. It was going to be a slow and difficult trek to the top. And we would have to leave our horses behind.

The climb was hard for many reasons. First of all, the slope was very steep. Second, many of the volcano's rocks were loose. It was tough to hold on to them in order to climb. Other rocks fell beside us, crashing below. We were quickly exhausted.

Hans was so much faster than us. He often disappeared behind a rocky overhang while we struggled to reach it. Hans would then give a sharp whistle so we'd know which way to follow.

Whenever we came to a small ledge, we wanted to stop. Even Uncle Liedenbrock was anxious to rest. He asked Hans if we could stop. Our guide shook his head no. He said something to my uncle, then pointed.

"Ah," Liedenbrock said. Then he explained to

me, "Look over there. Do you see the dust and sand swirling? It is coming this way. We need to get out of its path, and quickly. Hans says we need to keep climbing."

We followed Hans again. This likely danger gave us a new source of energy. Uncle and I climbed as quickly as we could. We decided to continue until we were safe at the summit of the volcano. It was almost midnight by the time we reached the top.

We quickly found shelter inside the mouth of the crater. There was a shelf about ten feet wide just below the lip. It was the perfect spot. We were sheltered from the wind, and it was safe and dry. I was very glad to lie down. This time, I had no nightmares. It was a deep and well-deserved sleep.

CHAPTER 9

Into the Volcano

I woke up in the morning, freezing. We were five thousand feet above the ground. It was very cold. I was not upset, though. The sun was shining so brightly that it put me in a good mood. I crawled outside our shelter and went to look at the view.

I saw valleys and more mountains. To my right, facing east, there were endless rows of glaciers. Their white and gray peaks cut into the sky. Looking west, there was the ocean. It felt like the whole world was below me. I had never seen a sight as magnificent as my view that morning.

My time of quiet thought ended when my uncle and Hans joined me. They paused for only a moment to admire the view. Then my uncle announced, "To the crater!"

He was ready to start going down right away. Hans and I reminded him that we needed breakfast. He listened to us, but he was not happy about it. He paused only long enough to quickly eat some bread and drink coffee. Then he prepared the ropes. Hans and I ate more slowly, enjoying our view.

Finally, we joined Uncle at the mouth of the crater. The crater was perhaps eight hundred feet wide. We all looked in. The sun lit everything, so it was easy to see down. I guessed the crater was about two thousand feet deep. The sides sloped in gently, and I guessed the bottom was five hundred feet wide. It didn't look like it would be too hard to climb down. We had good, strong equipment.

We tied our ropes to solid rocks at the top of the crater. Once the ropes were secure, we made our slow descent. Other than some loose rocks slipping past us, we reached the bottom without any trouble. It was midday when we touched the bottom of the crater.

I sat down on a rock and stared up at the sky. The mouth of the crater looked much smaller from far below. The sky was now gray. I watched as clouds swirled over the opening. I was surprisingly calm. I was not as scared as I thought I would be.

My uncle was not so relaxed. He raced around the crater floor. I had no idea how long I was staring at the sky. I had no idea how long he was examining the crater. I only became aware of him when he called my name.

"Axel! Axel!" he called. "Come here now. I need you!"

I rushed over as quickly as I could. He was

standing on a tall rock, looking up at something on the wall of the crater.

"Look at this!" he said. He pointed to writing on the rock. "Arne Saknussemm! Look, he was here. We were right!"

There was writing high on the wall. It was the same runes we found in Saknussemm's note.

I suddenly felt very tired. I looked over to Hans. He was sound asleep, tucked in close to some rocks. I thought this was a very good idea.

I picked up my pack and unrolled my blanket. I found my own sleeping spot and lay down. My uncle continued wandering and exploring as I went to sleep.

We woke up the next morning to gray skies. Right away I noticed my uncle was very angry. It took only a moment to understand the problem. There were three tunnels.

How would my uncle know which one to take? We did not have enough time or supplies to explore one only to discover it was the wrong choice. The note we found in the book said we would know which tunnel to choose by shadows. At the end of June, the sun would be in the right position to cast a shadow over the entrance of the correct tunnel.

But if there was no sun, then there would

be no shadow. With today's gray sky, there was nothing to do but wait.

Thankfully, the sun arrived the next day. It was June 28. We watched as its glorious rays filled the sky with golden light. The shadow worked its way down the side of the crater. We watched and waited. It landed right above one of the tunnel entrances.

Uncle Liedenbrock almost jumped for joy. I think he might have even clapped his hands.

"To the center of the Earth!" he cried. He picked up his pack and as much equipment as he could carry. That's when the real journey began. Hans and I organized the equipment and followed my uncle.

Before I entered the tunnel, I stopped. This was my last chance to turn back. I thought about my little Gräuben. I thought of her smile. I thought about seeing her again. And with that, I started on my way.

Hans helped my uncle down the tunnel to the next level. He slowly lowered the rope until Uncle Liedenbrock touched down. Hans then motioned that I should go next. I secured myself to the rope, just as my uncle had done. Hans helped lower me. When I reached my uncle, I helped Hans. I braced my feet against the rocks and held the rope tightly so it did not swing while Hans made his way down.

This first part of our journey was the hardest. As the tunnel continued, it became very steep. We had to move very carefully. It was as if we were climbing down a chimney. We used the ropes to steady ourselves while we lowered ourselves down the rock.

This was very difficult work, but I was interested in looking at the rock. I examined it as I passed by. The farther we went down, the older the rock was. It was as if we were moving back through the ages!

"The farther I go, the more confident I become," my uncle suddenly said. "I am sure that we are on the right path."

Hans called, and we understood that he wanted us to stop.

"What is going on?" I asked.

My uncle asked Hans to explain himself. "He says that we are here. We have reached the bottom."

"The bottom?" I asked. "But where do we go now? Is there nowhere else to go?"

Hans pointed to one side and said something to my uncle.

"He says there is another tunnel just past these rocks. But he wants to stop now for food and rest." My uncle sat down on a rock. "I have to say that I agree with him this time."

So we sat down and ate our dinner. Then we settled in for a good sleep. The journey would continue the next day.

CHAPTER 10

The First Sign of Trouble

ᗡ

When I opened my eyes, I was looking straight up the tunnel we had just climbed down. If I stood in the right spot, I could still see blue sky above. It was the perfect view.

"Well, Axel," my uncle said, "did you sleep well? I'd say it was a much better sleep than we'd have at home. No noise from the streets. No sounds from the market. It is very peaceful here, don't you think?"

"Well, we *are* deep underground," I said.

"Heavens no," he replied. "We have not even

61

reached ground level! We climbed five thousand feet to the top of the volcano. We have only gone down three thousand feet. We still have a long way to go."

In his journal Uncle Liedenbrock wrote down the temperature and the direction we were heading—whether south, east, west, or north. He did this every morning to record our progress. With that, we set off again.

Even though I could see a bit of the sky from here, we still needed extra light. Our lamps glowed against the sides of the tunnel. The last time this volcano had erupted, it was 1219. Boiling-hot lava passed through these corridors and coated the walls. They were now shiny as metal. We could see the different colors of the hardened lava.

"It's magnificent," I exclaimed. "Look, Uncle. I've never seen anything so incredible."

"I'm glad you are finally enjoying yourself,"

he said. "I knew you would be impressed once you stopped worrying."

As we continued on, I noticed that it was not getting hotter. Most theories said the center of the Earth was filled with hot gases. Although we were not far underground, I wondered when the temperature would start to change. My uncle took precise measurements so he could record any differences. I tried not to worry about this, either.

At 8 p.m., we sat down for our dinner. We had some bread and canned meat. I enjoyed my little bit of food. But I started to worry about something else. Water. Would we have enough water to get us through our journey?

I mentioned this fear to my uncle. He quieted me with a wave of his hand. "I am certain that we will find a stream along the way. We do not have to worry about our water supply."

This did little to calm my worries, but there

was no point in arguing. My uncle was sure of himself. I settled down for another night's sleep. All our activity was making me very tired by the end of each day.

The next morning, we began our journey again. We did not get too far before we had to stop. Our tunnel came to a chamber. There were two tunnels leading from it. We had no idea what to do.

Uncle Liedenbrock made a quick decision. He pointed to the tunnel on the right and headed inside. Hans and I followed.

As we walked, I noticed something strange. The rock formations were changing again. But this time they were getting newer, not older. We were not walking down. We were heading back up to the surface!

I pointed this out to my uncle, but he didn't listen. I think he did not want to admit that he had made the wrong choice.

"But Uncle," I said. "Haven't you noticed the tunnel is sloping upward? I'm sure we are going in the wrong direction."

"And I am sure that you are mistaken," he replied. We continued on.

"I'm worried about our water supply," I said a little while later. "We are already running short. If we go too far in the wrong direction, we won't have enough to survive."

"You worry too much," Uncle Liedenbrock said. "We will continue until we reach the end. We will not turn back. We will portion the water if necessary."

We continued on.

CHAPTER 11

Axel Struggles Against the Odds

∾

We drank our water with great care. We only had enough for three more days. My uncle thought we would find an underground stream. But I had a feeling that that was impossible. We were surrounded by hard lava rocks. I knew water could not break through to form an underground stream. I worried a lot.

We spent three long days walking in almost total silence. We had very little energy to do anything more than walk. At times, it felt like the tunnel was going downhill. I imagine that helped Uncle Liedenbrock feel a bit better about his choice. Perhaps that's what kept him on his mission. We continued for another two days before anything changed. We had been walking in the same direction for five days in total.

We had spent a long day walking. I started to notice that the tunnel walls were looking very different. They were no longer shiny and metallic. In fact, they looked quite dark. I put my hand against the wall, and it came back black.

"What is this all over my hand?" I said. "Look, it's all black." I held my hand out for the others to see.

"It's coal," he said. "We are in a coal mine."

"A coal mine?" I held my lamp higher to look around.

The tunnel suddenly opened up to another cavern. It was huge. I held the lamp up to look around me. The walls were lined with coal and layers of different rocks. I rushed to a wall so I could examine the rocks more carefully. I ran my hand along the wall, amazed at how smooth and perfect it felt.

I followed my uncle and Hans as they walked through the cavern. But I wasn't really paying attention. I was too busy looking up. It took me a few minutes to notice that my uncle was talking.

"Nothing at all," he said.

"Excuse me?" I replied. "Nothing? What do you mean?"

"We have reached the end," he said. "There is nowhere else to go from here. Well, this is disappointing. But at least I know now that this was not the correct route."

Hans laid out our meal. We decided we would stop here for a rest before heading back the way we came. We would need our energy.

"Uncle," I said. "Our water is almost gone. There are only a few drops left. And we are at least five days from the start of this tunnel. Are you saying we will have to go all that way back with no water?"

"We will survive on our courage," he said. I chose not to reply.

Once again, I did not sleep well. I worried all night long about our water supply. There was no way we could make it back in time. I woke up not feeling rested. We started heading back that morning.

Later that day we drank our last few drops. We were now completely without water.

We struggled through the tunnel. My throat was so dry, it burned. We were getting weaker and weaker.

By they end of the second day without water, I had to hold myself up against the wall for support. I was having trouble lifting my feet. By the end of the third day, we could not walk at all. All three of us crawled along the floor of the tunnel. We dragged our packs behind us. Finally, I could take no more. I collapsed. I lay flat against the ground, moving no more.

All voices sounded very far away. I heard my uncle talking to Hans, then felt him move nearer. He lifted my head and put it in his lap.

"My dear boy," he said. "Drink, Drink."

I thought perhaps my uncle had gone mad. Drink? What was I supposed to drink? He held his flask to my mouth and poured in a few drops of water.

A miracle!

He poured in a few more drops and I was restored. I looked up at my uncle. Were those tears in his eyes?

"How could it be?" I asked. "Where did the water come from?"

"I saved the last drink for you," he said. "Poor boy. I knew you would have a difficult time."

I was overwhelmed by this kindness. I knew

that my uncle cared for me. But I was surprised that he was being so gentle. He was normally so gruff. This action was very thoughtful, and I was touched.

I thought that now my uncle would understand my worries. I suggested that we go back to the surface to search for water.

"Go back?" he said. "Axel, did that drink of water not give you courage? We cannot turn back now."

"But Uncle," I pleaded, "without water, we will die."

"Fine!" he said. "You and Hans can leave. I will continue on my own."

"By yourself? Uncle, you can't make this journey on your own," I said.

"I intend to finish what I started," he said. "If I must go on my own, then I will."

I grabbed Hans by the arms and tried to drag him to his feet. "Hans," I said. "We must force him back! We cannot stay in this tunnel! We will all die!" My uncle refused to move.

"Axel," my uncle said. "Listen to me. I will make a deal with you."

I let go of Hans's arms and listened.

"While you were passed out, I explored a bit," he said. "We are very close to the other tunnel. I was able to climb up and look inside. That's how close we are. I saw that the other tunnel slopes right down at a steep angle. We will be on the right track again soon. Give me one more day. We will leave in the morning. If we don't find water by the end of the day, we will go back to the surface."

"Do you promise?" I asked.

"I promise," he said.

CHAPTER 12

The Search for Water Continues

∽

We set off again. Hans led the way as usual. We finally arrived back where we had started before my uncle chose the wrong tunnel. This time, we went left. The new tunnel began with a steep slope. We used the rope to get down the first part safely.

After that it was slow climbing downward. We moved along at a steady pace. Again, we were silent. None of us wanted to waste any energy on conversation. Even though no one—not even

I—mentioned it, we all worried about having no water.

The rest of the day passed in the same way. Walking, no talking, and no water. I was in a great deal of pain. It was getting harder and harder to walk upright. I was dizzy and had a terrible headache. Eventually, I could take it no more. I dropped to my knees and cried out.

"Help! I'm dying!" I held my head in my hands.

My uncle stopped and turned toward me. He looked truly angry.

"It is over!" he cried. "Our great journey is over before it even began."

I could not face my uncle and his anger. He seemed to be talking to himself. Whom was he angry with? I did not know and did not want to ask. So I closed my eyes and tried to sleep.

My uncle's words would not leave me, though. "It is over!" His outburst was about much more than our journey. We were already in a weakened state. Even if we turned back now, would we make it back to the surface of the Earth? My uncle was right. We would not make it out alive.

I slowly became aware of a sound. I opened my eyes and sat up. The tunnel was very dark, but I could hear Hans get up. He moved toward the sound. I tried to call out, but I could not speak. My throat was too dry. I was going mad. I was certain that Hans was leaving us.

I was relieved when I heard him walking back toward us.

He touched my uncle on the shoulder and said, *"Vatten."*

Even though I did not speak a word of Icelandic, I knew exactly what he had said: water. He found water!

"Where?" I said. I jumped up. Suddenly I felt no pain. I had new strength. We all grabbed our packs. We moved quickly through the tunnel. Hans led the way.

We walked for more than an hour and traveled about two thousand feet. The sound was getting louder. It was definitely water. I could hear it flowing behind the wall of rock.

"It's an underground river," Uncle Liedenbrock said. "I knew we would find one."

The sound of flowing water alone refreshed me. I pushed onward, and downward. I expected to see and feel water at any moment. Two hours later, though, we were still walking. We hadn't found any water yet.

Then Hans stopped. He turned and walked back a few feet. He put his ear up to the rock wall and listened. When he turned to look at us, he smiled.

I watched as our guide grabbed a pickax and swung with all his might. The ax hit the hard rock.

"What an excellent idea!" my uncle cried. "I never would have thought of it!"

I was so eager for the water that I forgot many things I had learned about geology. For instance, it's very dangerous to disturb rocks underground. I ignored this thought, though. It was more important for Hans to keep swinging.

It took more than an hour for Hans to break through the rock wall. At first, only a trickle of water came out. I worried that might be all. Suddenly the rocks burst away as the river of water broke free. Hans was nearly knocked to the ground with the blast. The water was boiling.

"It will cool down," Uncle Liedenbrock said.

He was right, once again. As soon as we were able, we drank and filled our flasks. The water tasted sweet and delicious.

We decided that our waterway needed a name. We named it Hans's Brook, after our exceptional guide.

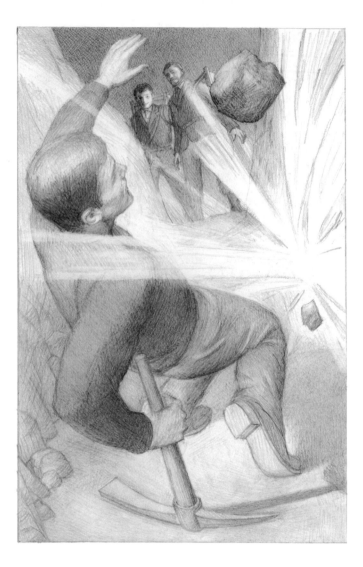

We were about to rebuild the wall of rocks to block off the water flow. But my uncle had a better idea.

"Let us leave it," he said. "It will travel downward and we can follow its natural course."

We picked up our gear and started off again. A small stream of water flowed along the tunnel by our feet.

We continued for several days in the same way. The tunnel was very steep, so it was slow walking for much of the time. Occasionally, it became so narrow that we had to crawl on our bellies.

Then, at last, we came to a new paradise.

CHAPTER 13

Axel Loses His Way

⌒

We passed through the tunnel and found ourselves in a beautiful cave. It was a wide, open space with a high ceiling. I placed my lantern on a rock so white that light filled the area. Even though we were far from the outdoors, I felt as if we were there. I took a deep breath and stretched my arms above my head. It was so nice not to be in a tight tunnel.

I could have stayed here for days. I hoped that Uncle was looking forward to a longer rest this time. While in the cave, Uncle Liedenbrock took his measurements.

"I have been very careful to take exact measurements," he assured me. "I recorded every turn, every angle, and every slope that we have passed over in the tunnel."

He worked in his book a few minutes. Then he said, "By my calculations, we have traveled 210 miles. We are forty miles underground."

"That means that where we are is deeper than the Atlantic Ocean," I exclaimed. "Forty miles! That is incredible! According to the theory about the center of the Earth being boiling hot, it should be more than fifteen hundred degrees right now."

"I know," my uncle said. He smiled. "It would seem that facts have destroyed that theory." My uncle seemed pleased to have proved my chosen theory wrong.

"Uncle," I said. "It has taken us twenty days to travel forty miles down. If we have an estimated four thousand miles to go, then this journey should take us approximately five and a half years."

My uncle looked at his book for a moment then slammed it shut.

"Enough!" he cried. "I will not continue with such nonsense. You can do all the calculations that you like. I have proof that a man—Saknussemm—made this journey on his own. I will do the same!" My uncle then left me and went to make camp in another part of the cave.

Two weeks passed. Every day was the same. We woke in darkness. Uncle Liedenbrock took his measurements. He recorded the date, time, temperature, and direction. We then walked through the tunnel until it was dinnertime. We stopped, ate our meal, and turned in for the night. The next morning, we started all over again.

I was starting to worry about our sanity. We were silent most of the time, left with our thoughts. People often go mad after a period of time like this. Maybe that would happen to us.

We moved in single file through the tunnel. We could still hear our underground river and used it as our guide. Having a water supply was necessary. Thankfully, we had enough canned and dried food to last for weeks.

On August 7, it was my turn to lead the group. I held one of the lamps and walked slowly. The rock formations along the wall were so interesting. I was paying more attention to them than to where I was going. At some point, I realized that I was alone.

Well, I thought. *I must have walked too fast. I'll go back and find them.*

I turned around and walked for fifteen minutes. But I saw no one. I called out, but no one answered. Then I started to panic.

Try to calm down, I said to myself. *There is only one path. There is nowhere else they can be.*

So I continued walking. Half an hour later, there was still no answer to my calls.

Fine, then, I told myself. *I cannot find them. But I can still go in the same direction. The stream will lead me to the same place they are going. I only need to follow the water. Eventually we will find each other.*

I raised my lamp high in order to see better. I looked along the floor, but there was nothing there. There was no stream! There was only dry rock and dirt. In my rush to find my uncle and Hans, I had not noticed that the sound of the water was gone. Now I was left alone and I didn't know which way to walk.

"There must have been another tunnel," I said out loud. "I was paying such close attention to the rock formation on the walls. I must have entered one tunnel while they went down the other tunnel."

My heart began to beat quickly, and my mouth was suddenly very dry. I looked to see if I had left tracks that I could trace back. There was nothing! I could make no imprints on the hard rock. I was seventy miles beneath the Earth's crust and feared I would never find my way out again.

My mind raced through the events of the past few weeks. I thought of Iceland and Professor Fridriksson. I remembered our boat ride across from Denmark. And then there was my little Gräuben. I would never see my love again. I cannot describe the amount of agony I felt at that moment.

Strangely, when I knew that I had no chance of survival, I became calm. There was little use in yelling and raging. There was nothing I could do. I knew that I had three days' worth of food, so I wouldn't starve. Not for a few days, anyway. This calm restored my energy.

I must go back up, I thought. *I will have to go up until I find the spot where I lost the stream. Then I can continue to follow the stream back up to the surface.*

I walked up the slope—up to freedom—with great determination. After about half an hour, I came to a dead stop. The tunnel ended. Somehow, I had walked down a completely different tunnel. Now I was hopelessly lost.

I turned quickly. I tried to race back the way I came, but I tripped. My lamp flew from my hand. I landed hard on the rocks. When the lamp hit the ground, it broke. I was left in total darkness.

I held out my hands, trying to feel my way along the walls of the tunnel. It was slow and painful. I fell many times. At last, I could go no farther. I collapsed into a ball, crying and moaning. After a few minutes, I passed out.

CHAPTER 14

Uncle Liedenbrock
and Hans to the Rescue

৲৯

I have no idea how long I was out. It could have been fifteen minutes or fifteen hours. With no light and no chronometer, I had no way to tell.

When I woke, my face was still wet with tears. I could feel blood on my forehead from the fall. I felt dizzy. I was not sure if I had the strength to get up.

What should I do? Is there even a point in trying to go on? I thought in despair. Then I heard a loud bang.

I struggled to sit up. The noise had shaken my whole body. Where could it have come from? Was it an explosion of gases down below? I listened carefully. I heard voices! I moved along the tunnel toward the voices. They were talking low and mumbling, but I could make out an occasional word.

"Hello!" I screamed. "Can you hear me? I am here!"

I waited and listened, but there was no reply. I leaned my ear against the rock. I tried to feel for vibrations. I continued to move toward where I had heard the sound come from. Low voices were still coming my way. Eventually, I heard my name. I was on the right track!

I realized that the sound was traveling best along the rocks. Leaning in close, I shouted as loudly as I could, "UNCLE LIEDENBROCK!" Then I put my ear against the wall and waited. After a few moments I heard a reply.

"Axel? My boy?" he said. "Is that you?"

It must have taken some time for the sound

to travel back and forth. This meant we were separated by a thick wall of rock. The following conversation took several minutes. We had to wait for each other's replies.

"Where are you, my boy?" Uncle Liedenbrock said.

"Lost," I replied. "In complete darkness!"

I felt a great mix of despair and relief. We had found each other, but I was not safe.

"Listen to my voice, Axel," he said. "Try to conserve your energy. We have been searching for you for some time. I have been worried sick.

"We traveled back and forth along this tunnel several times. We shot our flare guns, hoping you would hear us. I am glad that worked. Now we just have to find each other by following voices.

"Axel, I want you to say my name, then start to count. I will repeat your name as soon as I hear it. Stop counting when the sound of my voice reaches you."

I did as he asked. I called "Uncle Liedenbrock" and started counting. When my uncle's voice returned to me, I stopped.

"Forty seconds!" I called.

"Good!" Uncle Liedenbrock said. "This means that we are about four miles apart. Don't despair, Axel. We can easily cover this ground. Hans and I have found an open space that is the end of many tunnels. Your tunnel must lead here, too. Start walking down and you will find us. Now off you go, like a good fellow!"

I did just as my uncle said. I felt my way along the wall of the tunnel, walking downhill all the way. The slope started to get steeper. Eventually, I sat and let myself slide down. This made the journey much easier. Then I started to gain too much speed. I could not grip the walls to make myself slow down.

Suddenly, the tunnel turned straight down

and I dropped. I landed on the hard rock below and immediately passed out.

When I woke up, I was covered in warm blankets. My uncle was watching me. When he saw that I was awake, he let out a cry of joy.

"He's alive! He's alive!" he howled.

"Yes," I said in a weak voice.

My uncle hugged me tightly. "My boy," he said. "I was so worried."

I tried to look around me. I was tucked into a little nook where I could stay warm. My uncle put his hand to my chest when I tried to sit up.

"No, Axel, you must rest awhile longer," he said gently. "You have had a terrible fall. Take another day to feel better. I can explain everything to you then. We have many wonderful things to show you."

And with that, I went back to sleep. When I woke up the next morning, I felt strong enough to sit up. I looked around. We were in another cave. This one was much bigger and more impressive than the first. Then I noticed the strangest thing. I could feel a breeze on my face.

At first I thought that I was still dreaming. How could there be a breeze so far underground? Also, the cave was letting in a little light. It was more light than one lamp could provide. I was very confused. My uncle, seeing that I was awake, came to me.

"I imagine that you are very curious about your surroundings," he said. He was smiling.

"Yes," I replied. "Are we still underground? Did I sleep so long that we returned to the surface?"

My uncle laughed. "Heavens no, my boy," he chuckled. "Nothing of the sort has happened."

"I don't understand . . ."

"Nor do I," he said. "I can give you no explanation. You can see it for yourself when you are feeling stronger. I think you should wait till then to go out into the open air."

"Open air!" I exclaimed. "How can there be open air?" I started to stand up, but my uncle tried to stop me.

"No, my boy," he said. "The wind is quite strong. It might be too much for you."

I insisted he show me what he was talking about at once. He saw I would not take no for an answer. So he wrapped me in an extra blanket and we stepped out of the cave.

CHAPTER 15

The Liedenbrock Sea

ᑉᵔᕳ

We stood on the shore of an enormous sea! Water lapped against the sandy shore. The wind, as my uncle said, was quite strong. It felt wonderful. I had to close my eyes because the light was too bright. I was not used to it after being underground so long. Spray from the sea gently splashed my face.

My uncle stood beside me. "The light must be electrical. I cannot think of another possible source. Also, the light is different from sunlight.

It makes everything look sharper. You can see fine detail at a great distance."

My eyes adjusted to this new light. I saw that my uncle was right. I looked up toward the sky—or where the sky should be—and saw clouds. Great, fluffy gray clouds. The view was extraordinary.

"Hans is building a raft," Uncle Liedenbrock said. "We found wood and other materials down here. This is something else that I cannot explain. We will set sail tomorrow."

"Set sail?" I was shocked to hear this. "We are going to sail across this sea?"

"The Liedenbrock Sea," he corrected me, smiling. "And yes. What else would we do?"

I could find no reason to argue with him.

"Would you like to take a walk?" he asked.

We started a tour along the shore. I was amazed to find small trees, mushrooms growing in corners, and animal bones. I had no idea which animal the bones were from, but I recognized the plants. I knew them from fossils. These plants have been extinct for thousands of years.

Even with all these wonders, the place felt quiet and lonely. We were the only living creatures. Once again, I was filled with fear and excitement. My uncle, of course, felt no fear.

We set sail on August 13. We loaded all our bags and equipment onto our raft. It was six feet across and ten feet long. In the very center was a long pole that we used as a mast. Hans attached one of our blankets to the mast to make a sail.

As we were leaving the harbor, my uncle thought we should name it. He asked me to do it. I had the answer immediately.

"It is called Port Gräuben," I almost sighed.

My uncle wanted me to keep the ship's log. This meant that I would record the measurements for the day. I would write down all that we saw and did. It was a very important job. I was honored that my uncle trusted me to do it.

The ocean was so dark, it was almost black. I could not see more than a foot or two below the surface. Seaweed floated along the top in strands five or six feet long. I enjoyed looking at them.

Uncle Liedenbrock was very pleased with how quickly we were moving. "At this rate," he said, "we should be traveling seventy-five miles a day, or more."

On our first afternoon at sea, Hans dropped a fishing line over the side. It was only a short time later when he felt a tug. He pulled it in and found a fish attached to the end.

My uncle took the fish from Hans. He looked at it closely. Then he declared, "This is a species of fish that has been extinct for years. It's incredible!"

"Uncle," I said. "Look at its eyes."

"Its eyes? What are you talking about?" Uncle Liedenbrock looked at the fish more closely. "My word! It has no eyes," he declared. My uncle reasoned that the fish did not need to see anything. The ocean was black.

My thoughts started to drift. I thought about all the various creatures that had once lived and then died out. Seeing this ocean and its surroundings meant I knew how the world used to look. We were the only living beings to see this world.

CHAPTER 16

Creatures of the Deep

⌒

The days at sea passed with few adventures to report. The wind kept us at a steady pace. We had been sailing for four days, and still there was no sign of the opposite shore. I was beginning to wonder if this ocean was endless.

I also kept wondering what might be below us. Who knew what other creatures might live under the water's surface? It was incredible to think about. We could find new, undiscovered creatures, like that fish. Yet the sea was quiet.

As you might imagine, my uncle was

frustrated that there was still no sign of landing. I tried to cheer him up.

"But Uncle, we are moving so quickly," I reminded him.

"It is not our speed that is too small, but the ocean that is too big!" he said.

The only thing we had to pass the time was taking more measurements. My uncle attempted to take "soundings." To do so, he attached the end of a rope to one of the picks we had used for climbing down the rocks. Then he lowered it from the raft. The rope was two hundred fathoms long—that's eighteen hundred feet!—but it still did not hit the bottom.

It took time to pull the pick back onto the raft. When we finally lifted it from the water, Hans pointed out strange marks on the metal. I looked closely and was amazed by what I saw.

"Teeth!" I said. "There are teeth marks on the metal."

By the size of the teeth marks, it must have been a very large creature. The thought of this bothered me all day. It even bothered me at night while I was trying to sleep. It was too scary.

Less than two hours later, I was woken up by a terrible shock. The raft was being lifted into the air! We were held there for a moment, then thrown one hundred feet. We landed with a crash into the sea. Water rushed over the sides. Thankfully, the three of us were not thrown overboard. At that moment I understood why Hans had secured all our belongings to the raft.

"Did we hit land?" my uncle asked. He had also been asleep and was very confused. We were all stunned. We had no idea what had happened.

Hans pointed. There was a large black object bobbing up and down in the water.

"It looks like a giant porpoise," I said.

"And there!" my uncle cried. "It is a giant lizard! And a giant crocodile. Now it has disappeared.

Oh, where did it go? We'll need to describe that in our journal." My uncle was very excited.

"A whale!" he said. "Look, you can see water shooting out of its spout." At that moment two tall fountains of water shot up from the ocean's surface. A large black tail lifted up then crashed down, making a splash.

We were amazed. So many sea creatures had suddenly appeared. They were all huge. The smallest of them could easily have destroyed our raft in one bite.

Hans took control of the raft and tried to get us away from this danger. However, there were almost as many monsters on the other side of us. There was a giant tortoise that was forty feet wide and a snake at least thirty feet long. There was nowhere for us to go.

The tortoise and snake raced toward our raft. They turned just as they reached us. Everything happened so quickly that I'm not sure I can describe it. All the creatures disappeared, except for the enormous snake and crocodile. They were each coming at us from opposite sides, or so I thought.

The snake met up with the crocodile about two hundred yards away from us. There a terrible fight began. The two monsters grabbed ahold of each other. They began to wrestle, bite, and struggle.

I noticed that the other creatures—the tortoise, porpoise, and giant lizard—appeared and disappeared during the fight. I pointed this out to my uncle, but he shook his head. He was watching these events through his telescope. Therefore, he had a much better view than Hans and I.

"No," he said. "There are only two creatures. We were mistaken to think there were more."

"How could there be more?" I asked. "We saw all of them."

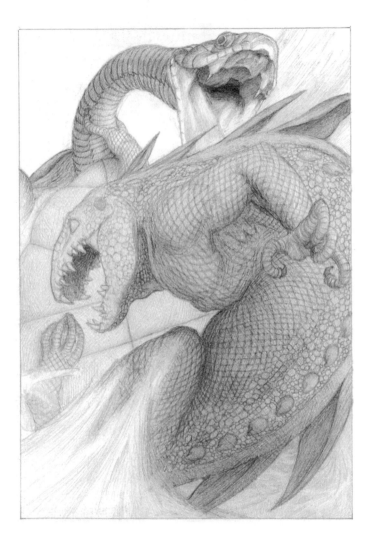

"One creature has the nose of a porpoise, the head of a lizard, and the teeth of a crocodile. The other creature has the head of a long snake tucked into the shell of a giant turtle."

As I watched them fight, I could see that my uncle was right. It *was* only two creatures. I watched them with great fascination. I was also terrified that they might turn their anger on us!

All of their fighting was creating great waves. Our little raft rocked back and forth. It almost flipped several times.

One hour, two hours passed. The fight did not slow down. We were still trapped in the middle of it. All at once the two creatures dove underwater and we were left with silence. Nothing. Not another sight or sound from these terrifying beasts.

CHAPTER 17

Passing Through a Violent Storm

A strong wind carried us away from the scene of the great fight. After that, our trip returned to the quiet, rather boring time it had been before we saw those great creatures. Once again, we were left with very little to do. The only change was in the temperature. It was starting to get warmer.

On August 20, we all heard something. It sounded like a long roar. Hans pulled himself to the top of the mast to get a look. He saw nothing.

Several hours passed and we kept hearing the roar. Hans climbed the mast again. This time, he stayed up there for a few minutes. He did not say anything. His eyes were fixed on one point on the horizon.

"He sees something," my uncle said.

"It would seem so," I replied.

At last, Hans climbed down and joined us. He pointed and said, *"Der nere!"*

"Over there?" asked Uncle Liedenbrock. He looked through his telescope.

"What is it?" I asked nervously.

"It looks like a tremendous wall of water rising above the waves," he said.

I wondered if it was another sea monster. "We should move toward the west, then, just in case," I said.

"Straight ahead," Uncle Liedenbrock said.

I looked to Hans, hoping that he would argue with my uncle. Once again, he did exactly what his boss told him to do. He guided our raft toward the "wall of water."

An hour or two later, we could see a large, black mass in front of us. I first thought that it was a giant whale. But then this was a whale like none I could ever imagine. It would have been a hundred times larger than any other whale. I was terrified to get so close. I knew it would not take much to tip our tiny raft.

However, this large, black mass did not move. Hans was the first to notice what it really was. He called it an island, and he was right. When I asked about the "wall of water," he replied, "Geyser."

Of course! It all made sense. I was rather embarrassed that I was frightened of an island! So I made sure I was the first to step off the raft.

It felt strange to stand on land after days at sea. I was dizzy for a moment, but recovered quickly. I helped my uncle off the raft then walked to the geyser. I stuck a thermometer in the rushing water. It was 163 degrees! There must have been a tremendous amount of heat below the surface of the tiny island. Maybe my uncle was wrong. The center of the Earth might actually be filled with boiling gases like I thought!

Uncle Liedenbrock did not care to discuss this with me. He wanted to get back on the raft as soon as possible. All he thought about was continuing our journey.

We camped on the island and set sail again the next morning. As always, we took our measurements first thing. By my uncle's calculations, we were now directly under Britain. He noted how many miles we had traveled and our southeast route.

The weather looked like it was about to change. The clouds were getting lower. I could feel more moisture in the air. Very soon it would start to rain.

"It looks as though we are going to have some bad weather," I said.

My uncle did not respond. He was in a terrible mood. He was angry that our trip was taking too long. Hans did not understand my words. He continued his work.

The wind died down, and the air felt very heavy. It was difficult to breathe. There was so much moisture in the air. It felt like sea spray across my face. The temperature suddenly rose. My clothes were sticking to my body.

"Uncle," I said. I tapped him on the shoulder. "I think a bad storm is coming. Look at the clouds. We should lower the sail and bring down the mast. If we hit a big storm, the mast might be damaged."

"No!" my uncle said. "A hundred times no! If we take the sail down, we will move even slower. We will never reach the other side." I almost expected him to stamp his foot in anger. I decided it was best to leave the matter alone.

Only a moment later, the sky turned black

and storm clouds rolled in. It started to pour. The wind picked up. The raft got knocked around in the powerful waves and we were all soaked. I never could imagine weather so awful. There was nothing to do but hang on.

It began to thunder, and lightning ripped through the sky. My uncle was thrown and almost tumbled over the side of the raft. I grabbed hold of his hand just in time. The seawater was almost boiling hot. Hail hit our raft and made a clinging sound as it struck.

The storm raged for four days. We all managed to stay on the raft. Thankfully, we did not lose any of our supplies. The noise was so loud that we could not talk. Our ears hurt from the crashing of the thunder and hail. The wail of the wind was deafening.

Our mast snapped in half and we lost our sail. It happened in a matter of seconds. There was a loud *crack* and suddenly the mast was flying away. We did not have much time to think about it, though. As we watched the mast soar off, we saw a much more frightening object in the sky.

The great storm mixed with the increasing heat. It produced a giant ball of gas and fire. We were terrified. All the elements were against us. We ducked as it shot past us and disappeared to the south. Then another one appeared. Then another. They left a smell of burned gas behind them. This made us all choke. Our eyes burned.

I tried to move, but I was trapped. At first I thought something had fallen on me. Then I realized it was the ball of gas and lightning. They had created a magnetic force. My boots had steel nails in the soles. My feet were stuck to the raft as if a large magnet held them down. I looked over and saw that my uncle and Hans were going through the same thing.

Then the balls of gases started to burst above our heads. Flames erupted and surrounded the raft. We were being rained upon by fire and water. All we could do was hang on and hope it would be over soon.

When the balls of gases and fire died down, the storm continued. Eventually, I could stay awake no longer. I fell into a deep sleep.

When I awoke again, we were on land. We had settled in a small, dry nook just off the beach. It was still raining, but the worst of the storm was over. Hans had pulled everything and everyone safely from the raft. Now he was preparing a meal for us. We ate, then slept. Tomorrow, we hoped, would be a better day.

We got our wish. The next day was wonderful. There was no rain. The sky was bright, and the wind was calm again.

Uncle Liedenbrock was bright and happy. We had at last reached shore. He felt much closer to his goal. He was ready for the next adventure.

But I was feeling sad. I felt very far away from

Gräuben. Every step meant moving farther away from home.

"Uncle," I said. "Can I ask you a question?"

He turned to look at me.

"How will we get home?" I asked.

"What? We haven't even arrived! Are you already thinking about the return?"

"I am just wondering," I said.

"It's very simple. We will either find a new path or we will walk back the way we came." He was not concerned in the least about how we would find our way home.

"But what about the raft? We'll have to repair it. And food? We don't have enough food to repeat the journey," I said.

Uncle Liedenbrock interrupted me. "Enough of this. We'll decide what to do and how to do it when we get to the end of our journey. We have no idea what we will find. You must learn to think on your feet, my boy."

He slapped me on the back. Then he walked out to the shore. I followed him. Hans had laid out the instruments and equipment to dry on the beach. It looked like nothing was lost. Even all our food was saved.

We sat down to breakfast. My uncle and I went over all our measurements. We figured out that we were about twenty-five hundred miles from where we'd started in Iceland. This meant we were now directly beneath the Mediterranean Sea. We also worked out that the Liedenbrock Sea was fifteen hundred miles across. It was a very impressive body of water.

"And now, let us find out our exact direction," Uncle Liedenbrock said. "Axel, please hand me the compass."

I found the compass. It was still in perfect condition, even after the storm. I handed it to my uncle.

He placed it on a flat rock, then looked at the

needle for a moment. He rubbed his eyes, then looked again. With a shocked look in his eyes, he turned to me.

"What's the matter?" I asked.

I looked down at the compass and was absolutely surprised. The needle was pointing south when it should have been pointing north! We must have been turned around during the violent storm. Rather than landing on the opposite shore of the sea, we were back on the shore where we'd started.

CHAPTER 18

A New World Discovered

～

My uncle was upset and very frustrated. After so much work and so many days traveling on the sea, we were back where we'd started. We did not cross the Liedenbrock Sea. We did not travel fifteen hundred miles. We were on the same shore, just farther down from where we'd set sail!

"Hans will rebuild the raft," he said. This was an order, and Hans did not argue. "It needs to be ready by tomorrow morning. We will leave right after breakfast."

Once my uncle had this plan, he was in a

better mood. "Wind, fire, water! They have all tried to keep me from my goal, but I will not be stopped. My courage is stronger than any of the elements! Stronger than nature itself."

I tried my best to talk my uncle out of this plan. I told him that the raft couldn't survive another storm. I told him that we might get lost again. And then there were the gigantic monsters living in the ocean. They might attack us next time we passed them.

Of course, my uncle did not listen to a single word. He walked back to see how Hans was doing. He had already finished the repairs and raised a new sail.

"Perfect," Uncle Liedenbrock said. "We will be ready to leave first thing in the morning."

Once again, I gave in to my uncle's decision.

"Now, my boy," he said. "We need to go exploring." We took flasks of water and set off.

We walked toward a wall of rock that was

about half a mile from shore. As we walked, I noticed enormous shells—some were fifteen feet long—along the waterfront. I also saw many fossils of old sea creatures among the rocks and shells. I figured out that the sea must have covered this area at one point in time. When the sea dropped down to where it was now located, it left many creatures on the shore.

We had followed the coast for about a mile when it suddenly changed. We started seeing different rocks, shells, and other things. Animal bones, large and small, covered the ground. All these bones represented thousands of years of animal life. There were so many, in fact, that we could not stop to look. It would have taken years to study and separate them all. But then Uncle Liedenbrock found one bone like none of the others.

"Axel," he called to me from across the beach. "Look! It's a prehistoric human skull!"

I took the skull from my uncle. He walked off farther down the shore as I was studying it. He had already spotted something else. It was another discovery, and just as exciting.

"Axel, there's more!" he called. "A prehistoric human skeleton."

I was by his side in a matter of seconds. It was, in fact, a full skeleton. My uncle was telling the truth. Neither of us knew what to say. What could explain this? Then we walked farther along the shore and found more.

"These are all skeletons of very primitive man," Uncle Liedenbrock said. "I would guess that they are thousands of years old. Perhaps they were here before man even existed in Europe? If only we could show these to other scientists. They really need to be studied."

We did not collect any of the bones, though. We could not carry them with us on our journey. There was only room for the essentials.

We followed the curve of the shore along the wall of rock. It led us into a cavern. For another half an hour, we walked along the cavern wall. The ocean disappeared behind us.

Within the cavern there was a wooded area. My uncle was leading the way. We came upon tall green trees and ferns dotting the cavern floor.

Suddenly I grabbed his arm and held him back. When he tried to speak, I put a finger to my mouth. This is how I told him to be quiet. I had seen something move in the trees. I had a feeling that we should be very careful.

And I was right! I pointed in the direction of the movement in the trees. We stopped to look more closely. We saw a mastodon—a giant, prehistoric beast!

Then we saw more of them. There was a whole herd. My uncle started to move toward the mastodons.

"Uncle," I shouted. "We need to keep our

distance. These creatures have never seen a human being before. We don't know how they might react to us."

"Never seen a human before?" he asked. "Well, what would you call that then?" He pointed to the edge of the clearing.

There was a man! He was herding the mastodons through the clearing. I could not believe what I saw. It was another example of prehistoric man, just like the bones. But this was a living example.

We did not want to disturb this scene, so we sat quietly and watched. After a few minutes, we turned back. We were too thrilled to walk back, though. We had to run. We were filled with so much excitement that we could not contain ourselves.

We reached the shore again to retrace our steps back to the raft. As we walked along, I studied the rocks and shells. Suddenly

something caught my eye. I reached down and picked up a rusted old knife.

"Uncle," I called. "What do you make of this?"

He took the knife and looked at it closely.

"Could we have dropped it earlier?" I asked.

"No," he said. "It is too old." He looked at it for a few moments. Then his eyes grew wide. "This knife is from the sixteenth century!"

"Is it?" I said. "How could a knife from the sixteenth century get here?"

"It's Saknussemm! This was his knife. He stood right here!" Uncle Liedenbrock started to look around him for more signs of the old explorer. Moving up and down the shore, he examined all the rocks. He did not say a word until he found what he was looking for.

"There it is!" he called. I ran toward him. He pointed to a mark on one of the rocks.

"a. s.—those are his initials. We must be on the right track again!"

My uncle changed his plan that instant. He decided that we would sail along the coast rather than cross the ocean again. Perhaps we could find other signs of Saknussemm.

The next morning, we sailed along the shore. We examined the rocks and cliff walls along the edge of the land. Four hours after we set off, my uncle spotted a tunnel within the rocks.

"Right there," he said. He pointed toward the tunnel. "We need to stop here and investigate."

We did just as my uncle commanded. Hans brought the raft to shore. We all climbed onto the rocks and headed toward the corridor. When we got closer, I realized why my uncle wanted to explore it. This wasn't a tunnel created by nature. It was man-made. It was created by some kind of explosive.

We walked into the opening, and Uncle Liedenbrock held up the lamp. The tunnel did not go far. It was blocked by a wall of fallen rock. We could go no farther.

"We're stuck!" I said. "We've finally reached the end."

"The end?" Uncle Liedenbrock said. "Do you think a rock wall stopped Saknussemm? Of course it didn't! It will not stop us, either."

"But how will we get through?" I asked.

"The same way that Saknussemm made this tunnel. We will blast our way through the rock," he said.

"We could cause a landslide. We could be crushed by falling rocks. We could—"

"No more excuses, Axel," Uncle Liedenbrock cut in. "Tomorrow morning we will blast our way through this rock. We will find our way to the center of the Earth!"

CHAPTER 19

Eruption

August 27. I will always remember this day as the most important on our journey. We had plans to blast a hole through a wall of rock in search of a tunnel to the center of the Earth.

It seemed that Uncle Liedenbrock had listened to some of my worries. He decided we could be in danger from falling rocks. So his new plan was to light the explosives, then gather on the raft. Hans would sail us out in the water. We would be at a safe distance when the explosion happened.

It was hard for any of us to sleep. By six in

the morning, we were all awake. We placed the dynamite in the tunnel and around the wall of fallen rocks. Hans made the final preparations for the raft. We were ready.

I asked to do the honor of lighting the fuse. While Hans and Uncle Liedenbrock waited at the shore, I went into the tunnel. I struck a match and held it to the fuse. It sputtered to life then caught fire. Quickly I turned and ran back to shore. I jumped aboard the raft and we set sail.

My uncle did the countdown from the raft.

"Five! Four! Three! Two! One . . . and go!"

I'm not sure if I heard the explosion. The first thing I noticed was that the rocks were changing. The wall was crumbling and then falling down, right before my eyes.

It took a moment for me to realize that the rocks were changing more than we expected. Too much of the wall was crumbling. A giant black hole was emerging. All of the rocks and cliffs on shore started to shake and crumble. The sea itself was starting to sway. Suddenly everything below us dropped.

The water dropped and our raft went with it.

The explosion opened up the rock into an abyss, this amazing depth. The sea began floating out into a big empty space. We were falling!

We all linked arms and clung to the raft. We had to hang on for dear life. Our raft sailed on the giant flood of water toward the tunnel, or where the tunnel used to be. We were plunged into darkness.

For a long time we could see nothing. All we knew was that we were all still there, on the raft. We traveled for hours through the darkness. At some point, Hans managed to light our last lamp. It flickered on and off, but gave enough light so we could look at our surroundings.

All I could see was rushing water. We were

floating on top of a wave. It did not look as if we would be stopping anytime soon.

We checked the supplies. We had lost everything but the compass and chronometer. The rope, hammers, pickaxes, and blankets were all gone. Very carefully, I moved across the raft on my belly to check our food supply. We only had enough left for one day.

We rode on the raft in silence. None of us had the energy to talk. The lamplight flickered once more, then went out. We were left in total darkness again.

To my horror, the raft started to move faster. We didn't seem to be gliding anymore. We were falling straight down! Hans, Uncle Liedenbrock, and I grabbed one another's hands and clung together. We landed at the bottom with a sudden stop. Then all of the water started falling on top of us.

There was so much water. It was coming

down too strong. I could not breathe. I felt like I was drowning! Thankfully, it only lasted a few seconds. My uncle, Hans, and I were still holding hands as the raft carried us off again.

We continued gliding along the water for a few hours more. It seemed as if we were in a tunnel again. The river was still quick, but it was much calmer now. There was complete darkness all around us. At some point, I don't know when, our motion changed.

"Do you feel that?" Uncle Liedenbrock whispered. "We're going up. We're starting to rise."

"How is that possible?" I said. I held my hand out. I could feel the rock wall as we passed. We were definitely rising.

"We must be on a geyser, or a spout," Uncle Liedenbrock said.

"But where will it take us?" I said.

"It's hard to say. We could be pushed out into another cavern. It could take us back to the outside world. But if the opening up top is not large enough, we could be crushed. It's impossible to say."

My uncle sounded so calm. He did not sound bothered or concerned about this. It all seemed to be just another part of the exploration. He would be a scientist until the very end. I, on the other hand, was feeling terribly anxious. While Uncle Liedenbrock found this unknown fascinating, I found it terrifying.

We decided to eat our last bit of food. Of course, I argued that we should conserve these last morsels. We did not know how long we would be on the raft. Uncle Liedenbrock argued that it was important to keep our strength up.

"Who knows what we may encounter on the next leg of our journey? We want to be at our very best," he said.

After eating, we lay down on the raft and rested. Each of us was lost in our own thoughts before we fell asleep. That night, I dreamed of my home and my love. It was a wonderful dream. I woke up feeling loved and missed. I hoped that Gräuben was well.

My uncle was already awake. He lit the flickering lamp and held it over his head. He was mumbling to himself and studying the rock wall as we passed by.

"We are definitely climbing. Look at the rocks. They are getting newer. It seems we are moving forward in time."

Even though we were climbing, the temperature was rising. As we moved away from the center of the Earth, it was getting hotter. I pointed this out to my uncle.

"How can that be?" my uncle asked. He was shaking his head.

"It feels like we are moving toward a fiery furnace," I said. "The water is boiling." It actually was bubbling as if it were on a stove.

I looked more closely at the walls. The rock was shaking. Cracks were forming. I looked at our compass. The needle was spinning out of control. I had to tell my uncle.

"I think that we are in trouble," I said. "Or should I say we are in *more* trouble. Look at the compass, the boiling water, and the cracks in the rock. I think we are in an earthquake!"

"An earthquake," Uncle Liedenbrock said. "I should hope not. I hope we are in something much greater than an earthquake!"

"Greater?" I said. "What do you mean?"

"We are in an eruption, my boy," he said. "I am certain we are in a volcano. And it is about to explode!"

We stopped, suddenly. The water dropped away beneath us. Our raft hung in midair, perfectly still.

CHAPTER 20

The Journey Ends

∽

I looked over the edge of the raft. I thought we might be caught on a shelf of rock. Perhaps our raft had blocked the flow of the eruption for a moment. I could see nothing unusual.

"Don't worry," my uncle said. "I'm sure this will be a short pause. We've only been waiting for five minutes. Our raft will start moving again soon."

Of course, Uncle Liedenbrock was right. In but a moment the raft started to shake violently. We all lay flat and held on. I could hear the sound of something rushing toward us. It was very, very hot. Even without looking below us, I knew it was not water.

Our raft suddenly shot up. We moved up through the tunnel so quickly I did not have time to think about what was happening. The temperature had become too much. The burning heat hurt my throat. My skin was red hot. I had trouble opening my eyes.

Bursts of fire shot past the sides of our raft. I could hear a deep rumbling coming up below us. It felt like the entire tunnel was shaking and might crumble around us.

"It is lava!" Uncle Liedenbrock shouted. "We are being pushed to the surface by lava. We are in the middle of a volcanic eruption!"

I cannot remember what happened over the next few hours. Our raft made stops and starts as we climbed higher and higher. The ride was rough and frightening. The heat was strong and

made me weak. I may have passed out during our last quick rise.

✧

The next thing I knew, all three of us were lying on the rocky side of a mountain. One of Hans's hands was on my belt. His other hand clutched my uncle's belt. I was bruised and slightly bloody. Otherwise, I was unhurt. I sat up and looked around me.

There was the blue sky. I could not believe it! It looked like heaven to me. It was absolutely perfect.

"Where are we?" I said. "Are we back in Iceland?"

"Iceland?" Hans said. He shook his head no.

"What does he mean, no?" my uncle cried.

"He must be wrong," I said.

I stood up to look at the other mountains

surrounding us. I expected to see ice caps and the rocky countryside of Iceland. Instead, I saw rolling hills of green, farmland, and houses. I could see small towns in the distance and lush forests.

I looked behind us to see the volcano. The crater was five hundred feet above us. Fire and lava were blasting from the top. Hot lava was flowing slowly down the mountainside toward us. We had to get moving right away.

We ran down the mountain as quickly as possible. Although we were uncomfortable and tired, we could not stop. We had to get away from the volcano.

It took us several hours to make our way down. We were always aware of where the lava was. We made sure it didn't get close to us. Thankfully, it was moving slowly. After an hour or two, we could not see it anymore. We did not slow down, though. We wanted to be off the volcano as quickly as possible. That was the only way to safety.

We finally reached the green fields several hundred yards from the base of the mountain. Then we decided it was time to rest. We found a comfortable spot under a tree by a path. Soon after, a small child wandered our way. We were very surprised to see him.

"You should ask him where we are," I said.

"That's a good idea," my uncle said. "But we don't know what language he speaks. The only thing we do know is that he does not speak Icelandic."

So my uncle tried speaking several languages to the child. He said, "Where are we?" in German, Danish, French, and Spanish. Only when he spoke Italian did the boy answer.

He said "Italia," then ran away.

Italy! We were in Italy. We had traveled all that distance underground. I could not believe our wonderful luck. We had started our journey in one volcano thousands of miles away in Iceland. It was incredible that we ended up shooting out of a volcano in Italy.

We ate a meal of fruit and nuts that we picked from surrounding trees. Then we headed off to a nearby farmhouse. We could find someone there to take us to the nearest train station. We would soon be home.

❦

I have now come to the end of our tale. We all made it home safely. We soon went back to our regular lives. Hans joined us in Hamburg for a while but he grew homesick. He boarded a train heading north to make his way back to Iceland. We hugged good-bye. I knew I would never meet a man like Hans again. I was sorry to see him go.

For me, it was wonderful to see Gräuben

again. Surviving our journey and the escape from the volcano was incredible. But it was not as exciting as seeing my love again. When we finally met, she wept and laughed at the same time. I hugged her as tightly as I could. I knew I would never let her go.

A few weeks after our return, Uncle Liedenbrock noticed something strange.

"The compass," he exclaimed. "Look, it is pointing in the wrong direction."

It was true! I took the compass from my uncle and saw that it was pointing south when it should have been pointing north.

"So we weren't turned around in the storm when we were on the Liedenbrock Sea," I said. "It must have been the electrical storm. It magnetized the compass and reversed the arrows."

Another mystery was solved. We had, in fact, crossed the underground sea. We did not get lost as we thought. This brought my uncle new excitement.

The news of our journey was soon known over the world. Uncle Liedenbrock became a very famous man. It was not only scientists who knew his name. He was known around the globe. His picture appeared in newspapers everywhere.

The story of our exploration, *Journey to the Center of the Earth*, became one of the most popular books in the world. It was translated into several languages and received rave reviews. Other people wanted to follow in our footsteps and make their own journeys. For me, though, I was happy to be home. I could think of no better place to be.

What Do *You* Think?
Questions for Discussion

ᴄ〜ᴐ

Have you ever been around a toddler who keeps asking the question "Why?" Does your teacher call on you in class with questions from your homework? Do your parents ask you about your day at the dinner table? We are always surrounded by questions that need a specific response. But is it possible to have a question with no right answer?

The following questions are about the book you just read. But this is not a quiz! They are designed to help you look at the people, places, and events in the story from different angles. These questions do not have specific answers. Instead, they might make you think of the story in a completely new way.

Think carefully about each question and enjoy discovering more about this classic story.

1. Uncle Liedenbrock is described as a stubborn man. What other words would you use to describe him? Do you know anyone like him?

2. How does Axel finally help Uncle Liedenbrock crack the code? Why does he do it? If you were Axel, would you have kept the meaning of the note to yourself, or told your uncle?

3. Would you want to go on a journey to the center of the Earth? What do you think it would be like? Do you think it would be like it's described in *Journey to the Center of the Earth*?

4. How does Gräuben help Axel to feel better

about his journey? Do you think she really wants him to go? Is there someone you like to talk to when you feel nervous about something?

5. Axel and Uncle Liedenbrock pack many tools and supplies to help them on their journey. What would you take with you if you were going on this journey with them? Is there anything special that you wouldn't want to leave home without?

6. Were you surprised that Uncle Liedenbrock saved the last drop of water for Axel? Why do you think he does this? What does this tell you about him? If you were Uncle Liedenbrock, would you have saved the last drink for Axel?

7. When Axel loses Uncle Liedenbrock and Hans, how does he react? Have you ever gotten lost before? How did you feel? How did you find your way back?

8. Throughout the journey, Axel tries to plan for the future and think about what could

go wrong. Uncle Liedenbrock prefers to focus on the present moment and take chances. Do you prefer to plan or to take chances? Can you think of a time when you planned ahead and your plan didn't work? Can you think of a time when you didn't have a plan and wished you had had one?

9. Even though their journey was difficult, do you think it was worth it for Uncle Liedenbrock, Axel, and Hans to go to the center of the Earth? Why? What did they discover?

10. What do you think Uncle Liedenbrock does after the story ends? Do you think he wants to plan another adventure or take a break for a while? What would you want to do if you were Uncle Liedenbrock?

A Note to Parents and Educators
By Arthur Pober, EdD

෨

First impressions are important.

Whether we are meeting new people, going to new places, or picking up a book unknown to us, first impressions can count for a lot. They can lead to warm, lasting memories or can make us shy away from future encounters.

Can you recall your own first impressions and earliest memories of reading the classics?

Do you remember wading through pages and pages of text to prepare for an exam? Or were you the child who hid under the blanket to read with a flashlight, joining forces with Robin Hood to save Maid Marian? Do you remember only how long it took you to read a lengthy novel such as *Little Women*? Or did you become best friends with the March sisters?

Even for a gifted young reader, getting through long chapters with dense language can easily become overwhelming and can obscure the richness of the story and its characters. Reading an abridged, newly crafted version of a classic novel can be the gentle introduction a child needs to explore the characters and story line without the frustrations of difficult vocabulary and complex themes.

Reading an abridged version of a classic novel gives the young reader a sense of independence and the satisfaction of finishing a "grown-up" book. And when a child is engaged with and inspired by a classic story, the tone is set for further exploration of the story's themes, characters, history, and details. As a child's reading skills advance, the desire to tackle the original, unabridged version of the story will naturally emerge.

If made accessible to young readers, these stories can become invaluable tools for understanding themselves in the context of their families and social environments. This is why the Classic Starts series includes questions that stimulate discussion regarding the impact and social relevance of the characters and stories today. These questions can foster lively conversations between children and their parents or teachers. When we look at the issues, values, and standards of past times in terms of how we live now, we can appreciate literature's classic tales in a very personal and engaging way.

Share your love of reading the classics with a young child, and introduce an imaginary world real enough to last a lifetime.

Dr. Arthur Pober, EdD

Dr. Arthur Pober has spent more than twenty years in the fields of early childhood and gifted education. He is the former principal of one of the world's oldest laboratory schools for gifted youngsters, Hunter College Elementary School, and former director of Magnet Schools for the Gifted and Talented for more than twenty-five thousand youngsters in New York City.

Dr. Pober is a recognized authority in the areas of media and child protection and is currently the U.S. representative to the European Institute for the Media and European Advertising Standards Alliance.

Explore these wonderful stories in our
Classic Starts™ Library.